Chris Karlsen's
Tasty Tidbits

Knights in Time Series
Dark Waters Series

Chris Karlsen

Copyright © 2013 Chris Karlsen

Books to Go Now Publication

All rights reserved.

Chris Karlsen

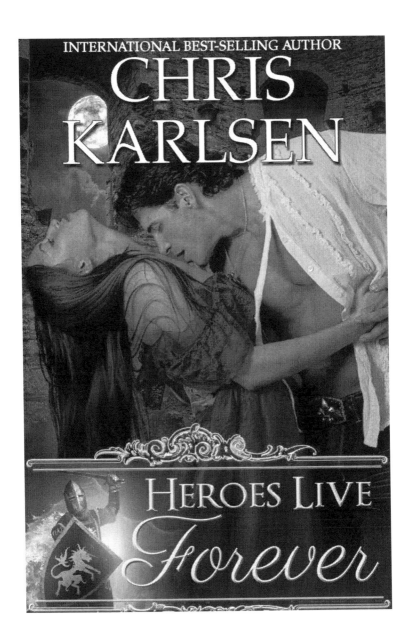

Chris Karlsen

Heroes Live Forever
Book 1
Knights in Time
Series

HEROES LIVE FOREVER

Elinor Hawthorne has inherited a house that is haunted by the ghosts of two medieval knights, Basil Manneville and Guy Guiscard. Basil is the man of her dreams, her knight in shining armor. She falls in love with him and he with her. Basil soon realizes she needs to live a normal life, a happy life with a mortal.

A lifetime later fate intervenes. Basil, still in love with Elinor, is told her spirit lives on in a young woman and is given another chance at life to find her.

Heroes Live Forever Excerpt 1

Chapter One

Badger Hollow Manor
Norfolk, England-1980

Elinor stood in the kitchen head cocked, and listened for another...scream? The sound cut off midstream. All was quiet upstairs.

"Nora, Nora, Nora!" Her friend, Lucy, hurried down the stairs and skidded to a halt in the doorway. Hand to her chest and wild-eyed, she gasped to catch her breath. "I've just seen a ghost!" Arms stretched out, she repeated, "Ghost!" Wild flipping hand motions accompanied the declaration, as if the gesture helped define the word.

"I suppose you think that's funny, screaming like that. I was about to run upstairs. I thought you'd hurt yourself."

"I'm not trying to be funny. I did see a ghost, a knight-like ghost...a Galahad-Lancelot ghost. Cross my heart and hope to die, if you'll pardon the expression. At least it looked like a ghost." She peered warily over her shoulder. "Oh, I don't know. It happened so fast."

Elinor looked too and saw nothing unusual. "Show me."

She followed Lucy up the dark oak staircase. Lucy twitched with every creak of the steps as they went. At the top, she paused. Elinor urged her forward and both women moved to the center of the small hallway.

"Where was this ghost, because, I don't see a thing," Elinor asked. Under her breath, she said, "I never do," as

Lucy went to the door of the master bedroom and stopped.

She huddled next to Elinor in the doorway and peered around.

"Go on, I'm right here," Elinor told her.

Lucy took a few tentative steps into room. She stood by the window which gave her a view of the bathroom too.

Elinor leaned against the doorjamb. "Well? Seems like a big nothing so far, no cold spots, no weird lights, no ectoplasmic figures."

As far back as she could remember Elinor was fascinated by spirits and karma. How many places had she stayed hoping to see a ghost and didn't? The Mermaid Inn in Rye, the Angel and Royal Hotel in Grantham, the Witchery in Edinburgh, all disappointed her. And now, her avowed non-believer friend claimed one appeared to her in Elinor's own home.

"I don't know," Lucy said at last and glanced around the room again. "I'm not sure what I saw."

"Did you see a ghost or not?" Elinor asked, unsure if she wanted Lucy, the cynic, to say yes.

A gust of wind ruffled the sheer curtain behind Lucy, the hem brushing her elbow. She screamed and bolted past Elinor, down the stairs.

"It's only the breeze," Elinor called after her, but Lucy continued her dash for the kitchen.

Unafraid, Elinor walked around the bedroom. She dragged her hands over the newly plastered walls as she circled the room. It had needed a brighter and fresher look. The paint and repair work on the house was one of the first things she did after inheriting the manor.

Elinor checked the bathroom and second bedroom. Like her bedroom, everything seemed normal. At the top of the stairs, goose bumps suddenly dotted her skin and the hair on her arms stood end. *Weird.* She glanced back, but didn't see anything strange, or more to the point, Lucy's ghost. She shrugged and continued down.

Chapter Two

"What the devil are you playing at?" Basil snapped.

"I was experimenting," Guy said, casually.

"Experimenting?"

"Yes. I thought our ghostly presence might be more acceptable to your Elinor if she had a glimpse or two of us first. Soften her up for the main event, as they say nowadays." Guy strode past Basil, not sparing him a second glance. "Revealing ourselves to her is your idea. I figured I'd contribute something too."

"How does scaring the life out of her friend soften her up?"

"It doesn't. I expected Elinor to come upstairs, not her friend," Guy added, in the same nonchalant tone. "I guessed wrong." He scrutinized Basil. "Since we're on the subject, I never asked your reasons for us befriending Theresa. It seemed harmless enough, she being an old widow, but why her granddaughter?"

Basil had anticipated the question when he'd approached Guy about making their presence known to Elinor's grandmother. Their previous experiences with mortals left them bitter. The women asked them to spy on their husbands or lovers. The men were worse. Driven by greed and lust for power, some wanted the knights to injure rivals, even commit murder on occasion and became belligerent when he and Guy refused. They avoided mortals for centuries as a result.

"I understood why you empathized with the loss of her son. He reminded you of Grevill," Guy said.

"Yes. When Clarence limped in and removed the metal brace from his leg, yes, I thought of my brother."

Basil recalled the pain her son hid from Theresa. The nights Clarence lay in bed doubled over from the cancer destroying his bones. "He must have known, or at least suspected, he was dying."

"Maybe...probably."

"I think, deep down, Theresa knew something was terribly wrong, that his illness was worse than he said. She may have even guessed he'd come home to die."

"Her mind might've acknowledged the possibility, but not her heart. What parent can bear the thought of losing a child?"

Basil nodded. "She started to fade after Clarence died."

Her desolation became Basil's and her loneliness his. A lonely ghost, God's teeth! He'd questioned how such a crazy phenomena could happen to him?

Basil gazed out from Elinor's bedroom window at the ruin of Castle Ashenwyck, his home in life. The remains of the former fortress lay not far in the distance. He focused on the sight and tried to find a way to describe the emptiness that filled him at the time.

"Over the years, did you ever miss human contact, the warmth mortals are capable of?"

When Guy didn't answer, Basil turned around. After a long pause, Guy finally admitted, "Yes, on rare occasions. Although, I never thought I would."

Basil shared the sentiment. "After so many centuries of self-imposed isolation, I grew tired of being a shadow. I longed for mortal companionship. It felt good to ease Theresa's solitude."

"And Elinor? Why pursue her friendship? At her age, I doubt she's lonely."

Basil didn't have a firm answer to explain the attraction Elinor held for him. "I enjoyed Theresa's company. I know you did too. I believe there's a lot of her in Elinor."

"Go on."

"I appreciate her kindness. She'd come upon Theresa, alone, or so it must have appeared, engrossed in an odd one-sided conversation. When in truth, she was chatting with us. Elinor never mocked her for talking to herself or acting strange. She accepted her as she was." Basil smiled as he remembered more about the encounters. "Sometimes, Elinor looked our way, and I swear she could see us, at least sense our presence."

Guy didn't look convinced. "You think engaging her friendship will be as pleasant as Theresa's?"

"I hope so. I dread having to remove ourselves into the shadows again."

Basil drifted out of the room, Guy right behind him.

"If you'd bothered to ask, before frightening the wits out of that Lucy woman, I'd have told you I already planned how to reveal ourselves." Basil tipped his head toward the stairs. "Shall we? Hopefully, we won't find Elinor's Lucy in hysterics," Basil said, as they descended.

Heroes Live Forever Excerpt 2

A man stood a few feet away. At least what was visible looked like a man. He appeared to be a knight, similar to the one in her favorite painting, except semi-transparent. He wore mail and a dark blue surcoat with a leopard embroidered on it in bronze silk. Tall, with shoulder length hair, in the soft lamplight, his eyes were as black as his hair.

"Milady..."

Heroes Live Forever Excerpt 3

He turned her around and untied he laces of her dress. His fingers lingered at each sliver of exposed skin the open laces left. The gown fell away from her shoulders and rough palms eased the sleeves down, freeing the arms. He inched the dress over her hips, unwrapping her like a gift, the silk pillowing at her feet like a bronze cloud.

Basil brought his lips to her ear. "I want to make love to you with each of my senses. I want to smell, inhale your scent," he told her and nuzzled her neck.

She tilted her head to give him full access to her throat.

"The perfume you wear, it is L'interdit, yes?"

"Yes."

"L'interdit." The word sounded almost holy when he spoke it. "I want to know where on your body the perfume lingers strong and where it grows faint. Here on your neck it is exotic and bold." He buried his face in her breasts. "Here it is tantalizing but distant." He knelt again. "I want to feel the intake of your breath when I touch you."

As he intended, she gasped softly as he dragged his tongue along her abdomen, blowing warm air in its wake.

5.0 out of 5 stars **A Most Different Story - Romance or Otherwise**

I truly believe I could love living with ghosts like these two. Good and funny characters and well developed plot. Couldn't stop reading but sorry when it ended. A totally different plot from the ordinary romance novel. A novel novel, if you will.

5.0 out of 5 stars **A fun romantic read**,

I enjoyed this book by Chris Karlsen. The characters were engaging and funny. Ian was my favorite character, I could read a whole series about what he did between his time of losing his true love and finding her once again.

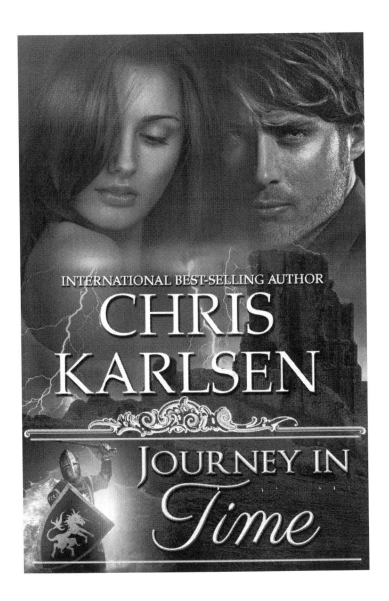

Chris Karlsen

Journey In Time

Book 2

Knights in Time

Series

JOURNEY IN TIME

London attorney, Shakira Constantine finally agrees to spend the day with her handsome client, Alex Lancaster. While riding in the countryside, the couple finds themselves caught in a time warp and transported back to the 14th century-and an England preparing for war. Everyone believes Alex is the Baron Guy Guisard, a baron who died in the upcoming battle.

If they can't find a way to return to the 21st Century, Alex will have to sail with the army to certain death. Shakira will be left alone to survive in the alien and terrifying medieval world.

Excerpt 1 from Journey in Time

Where did an Elysian Fields exist in England? Shakira knew of its origins in Greek mythology, but not anywhere else. Shortly into the ride, the answer loomed before her as a large Norman castle of Cotswold stone appeared. A crenellated curtain wall twenty-feet high and lined with evenly spaced arrow loop windows surrounded the structure. Towers stood at the gated entrance and armed men patrolled the palisades. One shouted from a corner flanking tower announcing their approach.

Alex dropped back to her side. "Remember, not a word."

"Yeah, yeah, yeah, I know."

"Give me your watch."

"Why?" It was her favorite Movado, part of their Museum Collection.

"Just do it."

She unfastened her watch and handed it to him. He slipped his off and put both in the pocket of his breeches. At the edge of the moat, he took her reins and led Eclipse over a wooden drawbridge. They crossed through a raised portcullis and into a vaulted passage on into the castle's bailey.

This had to be a movie set she assumed as they entered. She was familiar with the landmark buildings in the area. A fortress this size she'd have heard of or at least seen pictures of in books.

She scrutinized everything they passed for sound or camera hookups. Meutrieres were cut into the stone on each side of the archway they entered. The "murder holes" allowed the castle's defenders to pour all manner of materials, from boiling oil to sewage, onto attackers. The stonework throughout the passage looked aged and the details accurate. The set designers did an excellent job.

A three-story cylindrical Keep, like the Round Tower at Windsor, dominated the bailey. A wide stone staircase led up to massive oak doors on the second level. On the first level, broad barn style doors with iron locks stood on each side of the stairs. Typical features for a Norman castle. The production company must've spent a fortune on the construction, unless it was a facade. She'd yet to see technical equipment anywhere.

Their arrival stirred a flurry of activity and drew a group of men who also addressed Alex as Sir Guy. He dismounted and handed his horse to a young man who'd jogged up. Alex laid Eclipse's reins over the horse's neck and then gave Shakira's hand a light pat, "Stay here."

She had a million questions she didn't get the chance to ask before he rejoined the men they rode in with.

While he chatted with the others, she viewed the area with an eye out for reflection from the lens of a hidden camera. Everyone dressed in medieval fashion. They spoke in the same archaic way the knights did, using language straight out of Canterbury Tales.

A few of the people who came to greet Alex stayed gathered around. The acrid smell of sweat and animal urine burned her nostrils. The people standing near Eclipse reeked of body odor. The knights hadn't stunk and she'd been downwind of them. Her eyes watered as the odor wafted up and she resorted to breathing through her mouth. Whether the people were students or actors, stinking like they did took realism way too far.

In front of a three-sided booth, a stout, muscular man with a bushy salt-and-pepper beard hunched over a horse's hoof he held between his legs. Smoke rose as he fitted a hot shoe to a mare. After a few seconds, he dropped the mare's foot and set the shoe on an anvil, where he began to hammer and shape the metal. When he finished, the blacksmith dipped the glowing iron into a bucket of water. After the steam and sizzle subsided, he fit the shoe against the mare's hoof again.

A half-dozen similar structures lined the same wall. The stalls were reminiscent of carnival booths. Their work spaces were enveloped on three sides by heavy canvas flaps or in this case flimsy looking wood boards. Two men in the work areas next to the smithy huddled over something she couldn't see. On the opposite side of the bailey, school-age boys tended to horses and animals by a stable and pens.

She mulled over the possibility this wasn't a movie set but a re-enactment group that prides itself on realism. Tourists, especially Americans, love to feel they're experiencing the real thing.

No modern conveniences were visible, no electric tools, no hairdryers, or motorized vehicles. Understandable for a strict re-enactment group, some are rabid about "living the part." Where were the tour buses and the public restrooms? Surely the health requirements insisted on some type of toilet facilities. She scanned the area again. Only she and Alex wore modern clothes. Where were the tourists?

Nothing made sense. Whether it was a crazy university project, a period movie, or re-enactors too into their roles, she didn't care. This was not the weekend she envisioned. She wanted to leave. The atmosphere, the people, and the looks they gave her made her uneasy. She didn't know what was going on with Alex. Why did they keep calling him Guy? Why did he know everyone? Why had his manner suddenly grown so stiff and imperious? Why about this place made it so dangerous for them? She closed her eyes and tried to relax.

Someone clutched her left leg. Shakira squeaked and looked down. A grey-haired woman with pale rheumy eyes mumbled gibberish and stroked the boot.

"Where the deuce did you come from?"

The crone squeezed her calf then tugged on the boot.

"Stop it," Shakira whispered, violating Alex's order to stay silent. The woman continued to pester her, handling the boot, pressing her face against the leather upper. "Let go," Shakira barked in a low voice. She shoved her foot deep into the stirrup and tried to jerk her leg out of the woman's hands. Her heel banged against Eclipse who danced to the right. The crone followed, tightened her grip, and laughed exposing toothless black gums. Shakira pushed down harder on the metal foot rest and locked her ankle.

The knight Alex called Stephen broke from the group of men and came over. He efficiently, if unchivalrously, hooked a gauntleted hand under the old woman's upper arm and yanked hard. The woman yelped and released her hold as Stephen gave her a forceful shove away. The crone ranted at him, and then sneered at Shakira. She made a weird sign with her fingers, spit, and tottered off. Shakira had no idea what the hell that was about. Had the hag put some kind of curse on her or was it a ward against evil?

"Nutter," she mumbled.

Stephen walked on before she could inquire about the old lady's odd behavior.

She had enough.

Alex must've sensed her anxiety. He interrupted his

conversation and was at her side in a matter of seconds.

"I'll help you dismount." He took the reins from her firm grip and lifted her down to the ground. "Come." He offered his arm and tucked her hand in the crook of his elbow.

"No." She refused to move. "I want to go home."

He looked ill, *green around the gills,* like he was seasick.

"You can't."

Excerpt 2 from Journey in Time

She had to be on the grounds. She wouldn't venture far. He walked the corridors stopping anyone who might've seen her. He questioned the kitchen servants. None that day served her meals. No one had seen her since the previous night's banquet.

Alex returned to their chamber afraid something terrible happened. Worse, he had no idea who else to ask. A chill breeze blew through the window and whipped at this cloak. Shakira wouldn't leave the window open in this weather. Wherever she disappeared to, she left in a hurry. He noticed her clothing trunk missing. She didn't disappear on her own. Someone knew what happened. He rushed from the room determined to get the answer.

Chapter One

London

"It's late. I'd like to go," Alex said.

He avoided large events like this. He attended tonight out of obligation to a couple of his music clients who were part of the entertainment. Their performances over, he wanted to leave.

"Please, let's stay awhile longer. Please," Annabelle pleaded.

Next to him, she noted all the celebrities in the room. A former girlfriend, his interest in the voluptuous blonde waned months ago, but she'd badgered him into bringing her to the star-studded event. At first, he said no. She assured him she understood it wasn't a date. She only needed an escort. He gave in. Now, he wished he hadn't.

Flame undulated and shimmered in Alex's peripheral vision. He turned. A column of coppery silk came closer, stopping just beyond his reach. In a sea of sequined black dresses and flaunted cleavage, the lustrous dress was a burning match head in a vacuum.

The material clung and swayed with the movements of the wearer. Curiosity aroused, he scanned the lady from the tip of her matching high heels to her raven colored hair. Devoid of embellishment, the elegant gown's straight-cut neckline revealed only the woman's collarbone and the curve of her shoulders. A slit on one side ended mid-thigh where a slender leg periodically peeked out, then retreated into the shadows of the skirt.

The official photographer for the ball snapped shot after shot of various attendees, but not the lady in the fiery gown. Good, Alex thought, she's not a VIP's wife. He shifted his chair and tried to get a better view of her face. Twice, when she greeted someone, he caught her profile. Then, she continued on her path. She moved farther from sight, leaving him to guess if she was as lovely as he wanted her to be.

While Annabelle nattered away, he continued to track the mysterious lady in copper.

She stopped and spoke with an older man he'd seen before but didn't know. They exchanged a European style kiss and her lips brushed his cheeks. After a short conversation, she gave the man a quick hug and Alex finally saw her face.

Strong, high cheekbones and a firm jaw line balanced the full mouth and drew attention away from a long, narrow nose. Darker complected than most women in the room with a natural looking tawny color to her skin, Alex wondered if she was Arabian. What words described her? Exotic? Alluring? Both.

Her gaze slid from the man to the rest of the room. Light eyes surrounded by thick black lashes fixed on him as though she'd read his thoughts and sought the author.

Heat. Instantaneous and powerful, almost tangible, Alex smiled, savoring the feeling, the rush. The women in his life, came and went, some quicker than others. All held appeal for a time. None had this meteoric effect.

Annabelle interrupted his enjoyment. She'd seen a popular footballer at another table she wanted to chat up. If things went well, "who knows," she said with a demure shrug and left.

The orchestra played the first few notes of *Unchained Melody*. This might be his only chance to get the extraordinary woman alone. He made his way to where she stood with her back to him.

"May I have this dance?"

She turned and smiled. "Yes."

A stranger to her, etiquette dictated a mere touch of his palm to hers. He preferred to set his own standards. He wrapped her hand in his and pressed her palm to his chest. Her brows lifted a fraction but she allowed it. Her icy fingers were a marked contrast to the heat radiating through the silk of her gown.

Stray tendrils of her hair hung in soft waves around her face and tickled his cheek and jaw. Her perfume teased the senses, faint and suggestive. He fantasized where on her body it was strongest. Had she sprayed a fine mist and walked through, or had she dabbed it behind her knees, her ears? Did she dot tiny drops along her navel and lower? He imagined those chilly fingers touching warm breasts as they left a circle of scent.

The song was half over and they still hadn't spoken. Time was the enemy. In haste, his usually glib tongue failed him and he said the first thing that came to mind.

"Your perfume...what is it?" Alex gave himself a

mental kick. He'd wanted her name not the name of some silly perfume.

"Intuition."

An appropriate name if her intuition suggested something more than dancing with him.

Beneath the crystal chandelier, she arched a little and looked up with silvery-grey eyes. The faux candlelight formed a luminescent bead in the center of her bottom lip. On impulse, he lowered his head and brushed her mouth with a soft kiss. The kiss and the song ended simultaneously. She pulled away, studying him with an unreadable expression. Alex bent to kiss her again.

With gentle but firm pressure of her palm on his chest, she stopped him. She ran the pad of her thumb over his mouth, removing the traces of her lipstick.

"Don't get yourself in trouble, Mr. Lancaster."

Her eyes looked to a point beyond his shoulder. He twisted and saw Annabelle coming towards them. Before they were parted he turned to ask the mystery woman her name. She'd gone.

She knew him, not surprising since his picture often appeared in social and financial columns. Who was she? Intrigued, Alex determined he'd find out before the night was over.

Two hours passed and Alex had caught only a few glimpses of her as she talked to different people. Numerous times he tried to edge his way through the crush. Whenever he started to get close, she faded into the throng again. On several occasions, he was certain she'd seen him approach. The unsettling suspicion she was avoiding him flared, but he dismissed the possibility.

Earlier, Alex spotted Hassan Al-Ahmed, a Saudi business acquaintance. Hassan attended many charity events. If anyone knew her name, he would.

Alex found Hassan deep in conversation with a group of businessmen. He tapped him on the shoulder.

"Hassan, please excuse the interruption, may I have a moment, in private, please?"

They moved to a corner of the room.

"What can I do for you my friend?" Hassan asked.

"There's a lady in a copper dress here tonight, tall with black hair, looks a bit Middle Eastern--" Alex glanced around the room. "I don't see her at the moment."

"I know the woman you mean."

"Do you know her name by chance?"

Hassan shook his head. "Sorry. She attends these affairs on occasion but we've never been introduced."

"Didn't she tell you her name when you danced?"

"I didn't ask her when I had the chance." Hassan arched *a you must be losing your touch*, brow. Alex had no desire to go into a lengthy explanation. "Stupid. I know."

"I can tell you this. She always comes alone to these functions and always leaves close to midnight, rather like your Cinderella, yes?"

Alex nodded. "Except I'm not going to rely on her losing a shoe. I intend to catch the lady before she leaves."

"She's an elusive creature. You might find it easier

to catch the wind. I wish you luck."

It was almost midnight. The crowd had thinned to clusters of small groups near the dais. Alex scouted the best location to watch for his mystery woman. The end of the bar offered a view of the exit doors so he positioned himself in a shadowed area. On cue, the lady made her way towards the doors and into his line of sight.

He made his move. Half way to the exit, Arthur Snoad, a musician's agent, intercepted him. "Alex, we need to talk."

While Arthur rambled on about bad distribution policies, the doors opened briefly to reveal the lady standing at the curb.

Alex dodged more of Arthur's tedious questions and suggestions. "I'll consider your ideas. Call me Monday," he offered before he broke off and shot out the exit. He caught a whiff of Intuition and a flash of shiny skirt as the door to the limousine closed. Had she seen him? The darkened windows made it impossible to tell.

Who are you?

5.0 out of 5 stars **Great book!!,**

This review is from: Journey in Time (Paperback)

I love the amount of research that Chris invests in her books. She isn't just shooting from the hip here, she's taken her time and found things out.

This is the fourth book that I've read by Chris and I love them all. She has a way with characters and settings that I think transcends the genres or subgenres that she writes in. I think she would do just as well writing any form of fiction that is meant to reach out and touch the reader.

I loved the element of time travel here. It's done in a way that isn't boring and really makes you think about the situation, like "what if?"

Once again she gives you characters that you really want to know about. You want to find out what will happen to them. You invest in them, like they're friends. The setting is just as great as the first in the series as well.

Chris is truly gifted with words and I hope to see many more books from her.

I definitely recommend this book as a great read!

5.0 out of 5 stars **Traveling where?**,

Journey in Time (Knights in Time) (Kindle Edition)

I read the blurb for this book and knew I had to read it. Granted I have read this author's work in the past so I knew it would be great. I loaded the pdf copy to my Kindle and the format got messed up. I then loaded the format to my Nook same thing. I tried my iPad and iPhone same thing. When viewed the pdf file on my computer everything was fine. For some strange reason, that I have yet to figure out, I could only read this book on the computer. Well, sad to say my eyes could not stare at the computer screen reading this book. I emailed the tour company asking for a different format. Within a few hours, this wonderful author has gifted me a Kindle copy. Was I surprised, yes, but then again Chris is an amazing author that writes a fabulous tale.

If you enjoy historical or medieval romance then you really need to read this book. After reading, the above excerpt does not sway you to want this book then read on, I hope my review will. This book is about love that will travel the test of time. This love goes from present century back more than 600 years, turns around with a flash, and is back in the present.

I know many people do not like time-travel in their romance book however this is not your ordinary time-travel. This is not just one person ending up in some distance past not knowing anything. Two people have traveled together. He is originally from the past; while she has only lived in the future. Yes, I know you are wondering why I am rambling. Well, I truly loved this book. I read this book in about 5 hours. I know it would not of took me that long but I was working during that time also.

You are probably asking yourself why I loved this book. Well, today this author allowed me to travel from present time London to 14th century England and back. I could see everything the author described in the book. The horses, the keep, the King's court, everything, and I almost could smell the sweat from humans and horses. Yes, reading this book was great; the reader will leave the present in a flash and be in 14th century England. Who would not want to read something that will take them back in time? I know I did. What about you, will you read this book?

Chris I have read some of your work in the past but I have to say this is the best book by far. I do not know how you did it, but you took me on a journey I will not forget. Keep writing you have a talent that cannot be ignored. Thanks for an amazing read.

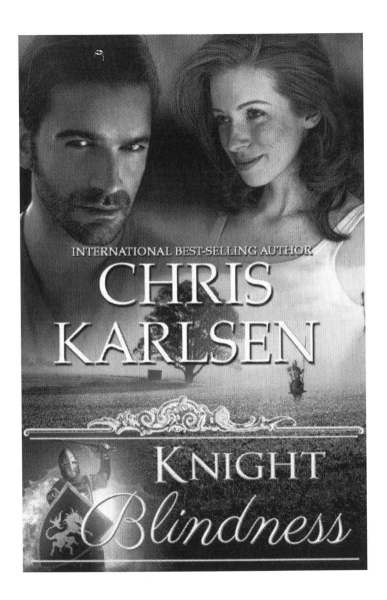

Knights in Time

Book 3

Knights in Time

Series

KNIGHT BLINDNESS

Ready for battle, Medieval English knight, Stephen Palmer, charges into the French enemy's cavalry line. Heeding a warning given months before, he hesitates as he comes face-to-face with the knight in the warning. Struck down in the year 1356, he finds himself landing in the year 2013.

Grievously wounded, he's taken to a nearby hospital. Confused by the new world surrounding him, he attempts to convince the staff he's from another time, only to find they think him mad.

Rescued by friends, who, to his surprise, have also come through time, he must find a way to function in this odd modern England. He is quickly enchanted by the kind Esme Crippen, the young woman hired to tutor him. She too is enchanted by him. Tempted to deepen the relationship, she hesitates thinking him adorable, but mad.

He must discover the means for getting her to believe the truth, all the while, unknown to him, he didn't come forward in time alone. The enemy knight has also traveled to 2013.

French noble, Roger Marchand, doesn't question why the English knight who charged him hesitated. That fraction of a pause gave him the advantage needed and he brought his sword down upon the Englishman's helmet hard, unhorsing the knight. He moved to finish the Englishman off when the world changed in a rush of sensations as he is ripped through time.

Seeking a reason for the terrible event, he enters a nearby chapel. There, thinking God has chosen him for a quest to turn French defeat that day in 1356 to victory, he sets out to find the English knight. The man he is convinced holds the key to time. If he returns to the day of the battle, he can warn his king of mistakes that snatched victory from them.

Excerpt 1 from Knight Blindness

Chapter One

Poitiers, France
September 19, 1356

Cries of the injured and dying French men-at-arms filled the air as Welsh bowman cut down the initial enemy onslaught. The vibration from the second charge toward the English lines traveled up through Arthur's powerful legs, the tremor slight against Stephen's armored calf.

"Be still," he ordered as the warhorse stamped his impatience.

His friend and baron he served, Guy Guiscard, said something indistinguishable over the noise.

Stephen leaned closer. "What?"

"We cannot hold them here, even on the high ground, not with their superior numbers."

Both eyed the grassy gap between theirs and the French held plateau. Unfurled enemy banners flapped in the breeze, a colorful swell that continued up the expanse.

"Maybe not but we can blanket the field with their blood," Stephen said, exchanging a smile with Guy.

Black-robed priests, who had earlier busied themselves blessing bows and swords now busied themselves taking confessions, offering prayers, and the Holy Eucharist. A decade before, at Crecy, he believed himself invincible—a young man's arrogant mantle. Today's hard battle would leave few unscathed. When the fattest of the churchmen approached, Stephen looked to the dying below. They'd prayed too. He turned to the priest and waved him off.

On the other rise, squires stood and took the reins from a contingent of French cavalry who'd dismounted. They retained their arming swords, axes, and morning stars. Behind them, line after line of mounted knights amassed on the grassy gap.

"They're saving the best horsemen for the initial cavalry charge," Stephen said.

He and Guy were in Edward of Woodstock--the Black Prince's column. They'd be the first to challenge the cavalry charge.

"I'm tired of watching the devils parade around foolishly thinking they cannot lose," Guy said.

Stephen flipped his visor down, the sound of the battle dimmed by the drone of his rapid breathing inside the steel helm. The waiting was worse than fighting. He glanced over at Prince Edward. "Let us be done with this. Give the order," he said low.

The prince straightened in his saddle as more of the enemy climbed the hill in front of their column. Then, the French cavalry charged. No longer a mere tremble of vibration, the ground quaked with the bruising the soft earth took from the oncoming horses. They rode over the men on foot and made for the breach in the hedge where Edward sat.

English arrows darkened the sky. A deafening roar rose from below as the arrows found their marks. Horses screamed as multiple shafts pierced their hides.

Those who didn't fall reared, bucking their riders off. Others bolted, crushing French and English alike.

Edward gave the signal. The prince's column charged into the butchery. Arthur slid on the grass wet from a lingering morning mist, blood, and the entrails of eviscerated horses and men. To Stephen's right, Basil Manneville, best friend to Guy, went down. His horse had taken an ax to the chest as Basil leaped the hedge.

Guy, several strides ahead, turned and rode to his aid. Stephen spun Arthur around, spurring him hard to help. His pursuit was cut off by a mounted enemy knight. The Frenchman came at him with his long sword, which Stephen maneuvered away from then quickly pivoted to engage.

The long sword was never his favored weapon and Stephen faced the knight with his shorter arming sword drawn. The Frenchman shielded his sword and drew his morning star. Trained by Stephen since he was a colt, Arthur didn't flinch or shy from the charge. He bared his teeth at Stephen's cue, ready to bite either the enemy or his horse. The Frenchman's mount danced to the left. The knight's position altered a fraction leaving a vulnerable space open under his arm between the back and breastplates of his armor.

Stephen plunged his sword deep into the Frenchman's side, striking ribs then soft tissue. The knight swung once with his morning star and then fell from his mount. The strike missed.

Several lengths off, enemy soldiers had Guy surrounded. As Stephen reversed direction to ride to his aid, he caught a flash of orange and black in his peripheral vision. Guy's warning from Yuletide the year before came back to him. *Beware the black cat in a field of orange.*

The image closed in on him. He turned and saw the Frenchman's surcoat, a panther on a background of orange silk. Stephen hesitated for a split second as the warning became real. The French knight raised his sword high. Stephen brought his up.

A second too late.

Excerpt 2 from Knight Blindness

Stephen woke from the dreamless sleep groggy. Since the Frenchmen took him from the field, he'd lost all sense of time. Bits and pieces of events faded in and out of memory. He recalled at one point he'd tried to fight and they'd stuck him with a small spiked weapon. It hadn't hurt, no more than a prick from a lady's sewing needle. Then, he was floating and had the sense of angels lifting him.

Not angels but his captors.

The delicious scent brought him awake. He might've slept hours or days, he didn't know. All he knew was the food smelled like fine fare and his stomach felt stuck to his backbone, he was so hungry. Those last weeks before the battle the army had run short of provisions. The knights had foraged for food along with their horses. The night before the battle he'd dined on overripe berries and dandelion soup. Soup indeed. Nothing but a handful of dandelion greens thrown into a kettle of boiling water.

"Is the food for me?" he'd asked, stomach rumbling.

A new man, one whose voice he'd never heard answered, "Yes."

He attempted to rise but tethers kept him prone. His wrists and ankles were tied to the bed with padded cuffs instead of chains. A small but curious kindness.

"How am I to eat it tethered as I am? Smell alone

will not get it to my stomach."

"I'll release you, but first you must promise not to fight or to touch your eye wrap."

"Yes, yes, I promise." He'd agree to most anything for a full belly.

Stephen sat up as soon as he was free.

The man put the tray of food on his lap and set cloth wrapped utensils into his palm.

"What is this?" Stephen poked the tined edge of a four-pronged eating tool to his fingertip.

"What is it? It's a fork. You know—for sticking your food with and bringing pieces to your mouth."

Seems silly. Why bother with cutting then sticking your food with the fork before bringing it to your mouth, an eating dagger is faster, more sensible? Stab and eat.

The aroma of meat and bread filled his nose and he put the fork aside. His head low to the tray, he shoveled the vegetables into his mouth with the spoon. A juicy, plump chicken breast nestled next to the vegetables. He tore the meat from the bone with his fingers, licking the buttery drippings from the tips as he devoured it. He last ate chicken in July and then it wasn't a fat hen but a wiry, tough rooster. When the spoon no longer scooped vegetables, he used his bread to wipe up any remaining morsels on the plate. The captors brought two more plates and he finished those before he was finally full.

Stephen sensed someone enter the room as the man left with the last tray.

"Who is there?"

"I'm here to give you a sponge bath, if you like," a

female, young by the sound of her said.

"You wish to bathe me?"

The pass of his hand over his hair told him somebody had washed it. No dried blood was caked anywhere. He sniffed his forearms. They smelled of soap and had also been cleaned. He had no need of a bath. The woman offered something other than a wash.

He smiled with knowledge. It had been a long time since he'd enjoyed the services of a bawd. Tempting as the harlot's offer was, he suspected enemy devilry and declined.

"Would you like to listen to music?" she asked.

The bawd traveled with minstrels. He wasn't in the mood for her other services, but he'd welcome a cheerful tune. "I would."

"What station do you wish," she asked.

"I don't understand."

"I'll turn it to a classical one."

A tune different from any he ever heard came from across the room. "I'll come back tomorrow," the bawd said. Her light footfalls told him she left.

Classical station? Lovelier than any minstrel's music, he dozed off still baffled by weird words and goings on of his captors. They'd woken him an unknown amount of time later and said it was the day and hour for his eye surgery. A man told him to make a fist. He said perfect when he found a vein and then stuck a needle into the crook of Stephen's elbow. That was the last he remembered.

"Monsieur, monsieur," a female voice said,

patting his hand. "Wake up."

Stephen yawned and propped himself up on an elbow. "Ugh." His mouth tasted like sour milk and his tongue felt like it was wrapped in a mitten. "I'd like some water."

"Here." The woman slid a flexible spout between his lips. "Suck."

He didn't know what the spout was made of, nor did he care. The water tasted sweet to his parched mouth and he sucked the cup dry. "More." When he'd sucked another cup dry, he asked. "What day is this?"

"September 22," the woman said, taking the empty cup.

Three days had passed since the battle. Why had they let him live? There could be no good reason for it.

"This is Dr. Berger. Do you remember me speaking to you two days ago about your eye surgery?"

"Yes."

"Dr. Monette is here too. We want to talk to you about the day they found you. The more we know about you, the more we can help."

"Who is the woman?" She didn't sound like the first woman, the one who smelled like a garden. This one carried no scent of any flower. Nor did she sound young as the bawd. What was this one's purpose? The first, he suspected, had created the potion that put him to sleep. He knew a bawd's.

"She is Nurse Cloutier."

Probably Witch Cloutier. "Ask what you will."

"What is your name?"

"Stephen Palmer."

"What's the last thing you remember before receiving your injury?"

"I am a knight in service to the Baron Guiscard. He rode to the aid of his friend. I saw your men surround the baron. They were trying to pull him from his mount. I was about to ride to his aid when one of your knights, his heraldic symbol was of a panther on a field of orange, challenged me." Stephen thought again how Guy's warning had made him falter. "I...I hesitated and your man struck with his sword."

"Monsieur Palmer, your eye injury is serious. If this answer is an attempt at humor, then it is a poor time to engage in such a jest."

"You asked what I remembered. I told you. I'm not in the habit of making jests with my enemies."

"Monsieur Palmer, we are not your enemy. We are not at war." A long moment passed and then Berger asked, "What year do you believe it to be?"

"The year of our Lord, 1356."

"Mon Dieu," Cloutier said in the background.

"From what the paramedics told us you said when they arrived, and your answer today, I am convinced that you do believe this is 1356. Monsieur Palmer," Berger covered Stephen's hand with his own. "The year is 2013."

Excerpt Three 3 from Knight Blindness

She knocked and a short, compact man with grey, thinning hair, cloudy blue eyes, and the reddest lips she'd ever seen on a man answered. In a way, he reminded her of Rupert Bear. He wore a red sweater vest over an open-collared white shirt, unfashionable brown plaid cuffed trousers that looked a size too big, and well-worn brown, wing-tipped shoes.

"You must be Esme Crippen." He gestured for her and Electra to come inside. He closed the door and extended his hand. "Will Davison."

"I'm Esme," she said, shaking his hand. "This is my sister, Electra."

"Electra, a fine literary name," Davison said as they shook hands.

Esme took a quick scan of the cluttered office, surprised a curator, even of a small museum, hadn't a secretary.

"You said you're looking for a drawing lent to us by the National Gallery in 1960. The Black Prince at Crecy, you said."

"Yes. Does it sound familiar?"

"I was an apprentice here then. I believe I know the work you're speaking of, an impressively detailed rendering considering the environment. It was done on vellum, we believe for the king, as colored inks were used, including gold, although no gold leaf was applied. We think the work was probably done by one of his priests. Unfortunately it was placed into storage back in the seventies and the facility burned to the ground in 1979."

The news sucked every ounce of energy from her. She had so much hope. Why didn't Davison tell her over the phone and save her the trip? The bloody drive took three hours. Bad enough to waste those hours not to mention they'd hit the London rush hour on the return. She'd like to wrap her hands around his scrawny neck and shake the fillings from his teeth.

"Fortunately," he continued, "We had a copy made prior to the drawing going into storage. "The original was fragile, obviously. The curator and I worried it might deteriorate more if it stayed on display. As the Black Prince was the subject, and is such a big part of Canterbury's history, we did want to keep a representation exhibited. We had it copied in oil. It hangs in the main room of the museum. Come, I'll show you."

He led them to a side door of his office that also served as a door to the rear of the museum proper. This section of the museum displayed artifacts and pictures from the Victorian period up to and including the hard fought air war, the Battle of Britain.

Through another archway to the next room, Davison led them to a painting. The gilded-framed oil was about a meter wide and a half meter high and hung in the center of one wall.

"Remarkable isn't it?" he said. "It depicts the aftermath of the battle. This is where the young prince raised up so many young men who fought alongside him to knighthood."

"Oh my God," Esme whispered. Shocked, she stared unable to take her eyes from the painting. How could this be? Identical down to the wound on the chin. She'd seen the scar on Stephen's chin up close.

Unlike the larger, more famous sister institutions, the simpler Museum of Canterbury didn't employ infrared protective alarms that go off when a visitor gets too close to an exhibit.

Davison's hand on her arm stopped Esme as she stepped forward, fingers inches from the canvas. "No touching allowed, Ms. Crippen," he warned and removed his hand.

"Sorry," she said, moving back to drop onto the bench in front of the painting.

"What is it?" Electra asked.

"Are you ill, my dear?" Davison asked.

She shook her head, too numb to speak.

Electra joined her on the bench. "You look like you're going to faint. You're white as a ghost."

"Would you like some water, Miss Crippen?"

Finally, she found her voice. "No. Thank you but I'm fine," she told Electra and Davison.

Esme turned from the painting to ask, "Is this an exact copy of the original?"

"Yes. The curator at the time was meticulous man and would not approve even the slightest deviation."

"You're positive?"

He nodded. "Very."

"Esme—"

She held up her hand to stop Electra's question. "Thank you, Mr. Davison. This is more than I expected when I asked about the drawing. If it's all right, I'd like a few minutes more to appreciate the excellent artistry."

"No worries, Miss Crippen. If you require no more of me, I'm going to return to my office. Take as much time as you like. The museum is open until five." Davison gave each a polite tip of his head and left.

As soon as he was out of the room, Electra said, "Esme talk to me. There's something up with you and this painting. I want to know what."

"The young man kneeling, two over from the prince's left, the one holding a bloody gauntleted hand under his chin."

"What about him?"

"He looks just like Stephen."

From Electra's sour expression, she found the explanation anticlimactic. "That's all? Jeez, I thought it was something really big."

"You don't understand. He could be Stephen's double. That's not all. The man standing behind him I'd swear is Alex Lancaster. A younger version but hand to heart, I think it's him."

"I've only seen pictures of Alex Lancaster when he's been in the press. I agree. It does look like him. But it isn't either Stephen or Alex since those men," she tipped her chin toward the painting, "lived close to seven hundred years ago. Why are you weirding out?"

Esme ignored the question. Too many of her own occupied her thoughts. How had his face wound up on this medieval man: the narrow too long nose, the strong jaw, the broad forehead, even the shape of his eyes...his injury didn't change the slight downward tip to the outside corners?

"Hello," Electra waved her hand in front of Esme's face.

"Stop it." She dug her cell phone out. Conscious of how light and shadow might affect the shots, she took pictures of the painting from different angles.

Electra tugged on her arm, pulling the camera away from her face. "He's not Stephen. Maybe he's his ancestor, five-hundred times removed, but he's not Stephen." She let out a heavy sigh.

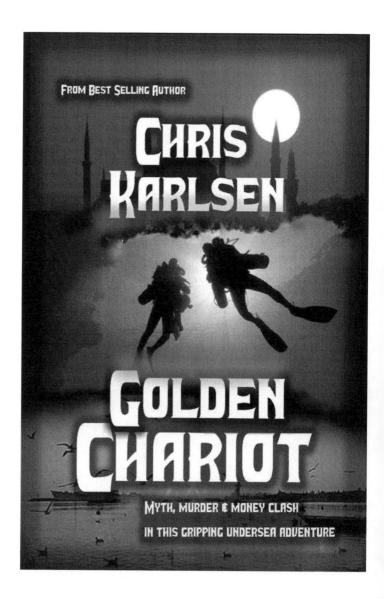

Golden Chariot
Book 1
Dark Water Series

Golden Chariot

The rare discovery of a ship sunk during the time of the Trojan War has been found off the coast of Turkey, near Troy. Charlotte Dashiell is an American nautical archaeologist and thrilled to be part of the recovery team. The wreck may contain proof of her highly controversial theory about the Trojan War.

Charlotte is present when the Turkish government agent assigned to guard the site is murdered. Her possible involvement and a questionable connection to a private collector of black market relics bring her under suspicion. Atakan Vadim is the Turkish agent sent to investigate her. Unknown to either of them, the smuggler behind the murder plans to steal a valuable artifact and frame Charlotte for the theft...after they murder her.

Excerpt 1 from Golden Chariot

Shouts of "fire" came from all sides of the camp. The west wind blew sparks in the direction of the lab. They could lose the entire camp, but not the lab, not the artifacts.

Charlotte grabbed an empty barrel from the fire line. She ran with it and started climbing the stairs to the shower stall's water tank. A man's large hand covered her mouth. His other hand brandished a gun. With the cold barrel to her ear, he walked her backwards down the few steps to the ground.

"Don't scream." Little-by-little his palm came away from her mouth.

Chapter Sixty-Seven

Charlotte searched and couldn't find Atakan. The schedule showed her diving with Gerard again. Atakan and the "pottery experts" had stayed in camp for the last two days. Refik assigned them lab work while they waited for Ursula to make her move. Charlotte wanted to see if Atakan and the "experts" would like to have breakfast together before she had to leave. She went to Refik's office to ask if he knew where Atakan was.

She knocked. "Refik?"

"Come in."

Refik had the steel box with the broken lock and its relics on his desk. He was bent trying to arrange room in his office safe for the added artifacts.

Charlotte walked to the desk and fingered the broken lock. "Ursula's work?"

"Yes. Atakan and his agents are in pursuit of her now."

"Is Damla with her?"

"I don't know. Atakan, the agents, and Ursula were already gone when I awoke. He had the Director call early and inform me of the circumstance."

Guilt swamped Charlotte. She meant to tell Atakan she was as worried for his safety as he was hers. She meant to tell him be careful, don't take unnecessary risks. Nick's SWAT escapades were bad enough to deal with. The time never seemed right to tell Atakan. A pathetic excuse.

"Hand me the pieces, please," Refik said.

Charlotte gave him the larger diptych first then the smaller pieces. Refik worked on his hands and knees wedging them into the safe.

Shouts and yells came from all sides of the camp as Talat threw open the office door. "Fire."

Refik hurried to shut the safe. The three rushed from the office.

The backside of the kitchen and dining hall was an inferno. Fire consumed the framing posts and spread to the plywood walls. The summer sun had dried the inexpensive wood they used for the construction of all the buildings, making the supports like matchsticks. Where the fire had broken through the walls, flames were sucked inside and started to engulf the tables and chairs. The grass matting used for the roof was next.

The west wind blew sparks in the direction of the lab. They could lose the entire camp, but not the lab, not the artifacts.

By a stroke of luck, the Suraya was still docked and everyone was in camp. They broke up into groups. One brought stored water from different parts of the compound. The others formed fire lines, passing buckets of water hand-over-hand, dousing the flames. Rachel ran to the village where the locals kept a water truck filled for fire emergencies.

Charlotte and Uma dragged a water barrel that normally served to fill desalination tanks.

"The lab," Uma yelled as they ran back for the second barrel.

Embers caught in the breeze had begun to land on the canvas roof. Charlotte shouted for Talat and Gerard. The two men took over handling the second water barrel. Charlotte and Uma ran to the lab and began moving cabinets and tanks of artifacts out to the open area of the camp.

"Dump the water tank for the showers," Refik ordered, taking Charlotte's place.

She nodded and grabbed an empty barrel from the fire line and ran with it to the showers. She positioned it against the back of the shower stall and started climbing the steps. Metal clamps on the side fastened the tank to crossbeam posts. Once the clamps were unhooked, she'd turn the tank and unscrew the top to let the water run into the barrel.

A loud whoosh came from the kitchen and a tall, black plume of smoke shot skyward. The roof was aflame.

She hesitated midway on the stairs at the sight.

A man's large hand covered her mouth. His other hand brandished a gun.

With the cold barrel to her ear, he walked her backwards down the few steps to the ground.

"Don't scream."

Little-by-little his palm came away from her mouth.

She screamed and tried to break and run. She spun as he caught her by the arm and backhanded her across the cheek with a closed fist. Dazed, she staggered but stayed on her feet.

A second man wrapped his forearm around her throat and covered her mouth with his other hand.

Tischenko stepped in front of her. "Your screams won't be heard. As you can see and hear..." He gestured to the burning kitchen. "Folks are busy elsewhere."

The second man's fleshy fingers forced her lips apart and pressed against her teeth. She managed to part her teeth the fraction she needed and bit down hard, drawing blood. He jerked his hand from her mouth but not his arm from her throat. He tightened the choke hold, cutting off most of the air to her lungs. Screaming was impossible.

Long ago, Nick told her, "If the only weapon you have is your body, then you make every move count." He showed her good pain points to strike.

She stomped her heel down on the man's foot. He relaxed the pressure on her throat. The distraction enabled her to wedge her hands under the man's forearm. She pushed with all her strength to loosen his hold.

Tischenko backhanded her again. Stars filled her vision then faded.

"You recognize me?" Tischenko asked.

She nodded.

"I will tell my associate to let you speak if you do not try to scream."

She opened her mouth ready to scream again.

"If you disobey, I will have Atakan tortured."

The mention of Atakan stunned Charlotte into silence. Tischenko had Atakan? How? She knew he'd left with two other agents. Tischenko overpowered all three? She didn't believe him.

"Liar," she rasped.

"Bring her," Tischenko told the man holding her.

Tischenko covered the rocky path on the camp's edge in several long strides. Her captor half carried, half dragged her along as she fought to break free.

Tischenko stopped behind a clump of trees between the rear of the living quarters and the cove.

"You can continue to fight or come along like a good girl."

Charlotte's father always said; *never go willing with a kidnapper. Never. You're better off forcing his hand there and then. He might kill you. He might not. But, if you go with him, you're dead. In all likelihood, you'll be tortured for hours or even days before he kills you. Go down fighting first.*

"I'm not going anywhere with you."

"Then I'll kill your lover slowly. I'll record his screams for you to hear. I'll record him begging for death."

Tischenko pulled a hunting knife from a calf pocket on his cargo pants and unsheathed it. He stood in front of her and put the tip of the blade to the corner of her eye.

"First I will take his eyes so he cannot see what torture is next, only anticipate it. Then," Tischenko moved the knife to the first knuckle of her forefinger. "I will snip his fingers off." He slid the blade across her finger, lightly, just enough to draw a thin line of blood. "One knuckle at a time."

Charlotte's body tensed and she clamped her teeth together. She concentrated on him, not on the sharp pain.

He moved to her second knuckle. "If he were to live, which he won't, he wouldn't be able to wipe his ass," he said, chuckling.

She couldn't contain her fear. It controlled her breathing which came in short, rapid pants. She winced, but refused to look away. She wouldn't give him the additional victory of seeing her terror as he made another light slice.

"Next, I will castrate him, one ball, then the other, then a final whack and he is a woman. In the end, I will disembowel him and lay his intestines on his chest. You'd be surprised how long you can live with your guts spilled."

A wave of nausea came and went with the picture he painted.

"I don't believe you. You don't have Atakan," she challenged, trying not to sound terrified.

He sheathed the knife and shoved it back into his pocket. From his shirt pocket, he took out a Thuraya cell phone.

"Atakan's phone," he said, showing her the face.

"Bullshit, anyone can order that phone on the internet."

"Such belligerence. I'm going to enjoy breaking you. This is Atakan's security code." Tischenko punched in a four digit sequence that was Damla's code.

Charlotte racked her brain to remember if Atakan used a security code when he made calls. She hadn't paid attention.

Tischenko put the phone near her ear.

She listened as Atakan talked to the Director. On another he spoke to someone at the Ministry about a report. Tischenko let her listen to call after call.

He has Atakan. She felt ill again.

"You'll kill him, whether I go or not." If he denied it, she'd know he was lying.

"True. Come, and I'll let him keep his eyes and manhood."

She had to go. If nothing else, it bought Atakan more time. If he wasn't incapacitated, maybe, just maybe, she and Atakan could find a way to escape.

"I'll go."

5.0 out of 5 stars **Must read**

This review is from: Golden Chariot (Kindle Edition)

Chris takes us to Turkey in "Golden Chariot". A fast paced, action packed, murder mystery with characters are strong and interesting. With romance thrown into the story you will find it hard to put down. Recommended to all who love the excitement of romance and murder thrown together.

Romance and mystery combined, this book was a great read!,

This review is from: Golden Chariot (Kindle Edition)

Charlotte is an American archaeologist, who wishes to prove an interesting theory about Trojan Wars. She travels to the Turkish Coast and caught in a shipwreck..not only that, but also she becomes the prime suspect to the murder that takes place in that ship. Atakan is the male, who is responsible to investigate that murder. He was annoyingly suspicious on Charlotte at first. But, when Atakan knows that Charlotte is not behind the murder, the attraction between the couple grow. Yeah, there is romance and its good. Will Atakan be able to bring the real murderers, saving Charlotte? Is Charlotte's interesting theory true?

Charlotte and Atakan's adventures in undersea are really cool stuff and their discovery of Troy's and Trojan War's artifacts are really amusing. The character formation and dialogue writing was so good. Although I am new to the author, this author is one of those talents that I missed out. The Trojan War facts are interesting to read and felt like reading one of Dan Brown's.

Romance and mystery combined, this book was a great read!

Chris Karlsen

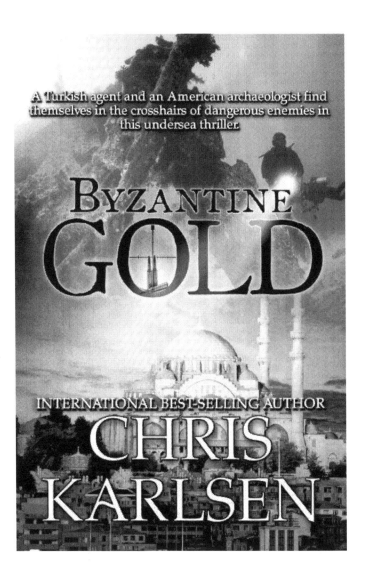

Chris Karlsen

Byzantine Gold
Book 2
Dark Water Series

BYZANTINE GOLD

A sunken warship from the Byzantine Era carrying an unusual cargo of gold has been found off the coast of Northern Cyprus. News of the valuable cache has attracted the attention of a terrorist cell. They plan to attack the recovery team's campsite and steal the artifacts. On the Black Market, the sale of the relics will buy them additional weapons.

Charlotte Dashiell, an American archaeologist, and her lover, Atakan Vadim, a Turkish government agent, are scheduled to be part of the recovery team that brings up the artifacts. While en route to Cyprus, they find themselves caught in the crosshairs of Maksym Tischenko, a Ukrainian contract killer bent on revenge. Charlotte, Atakan and Tischenko share a grim history. As a result, Tischenko is a man who will stop at nothing to achieve his goal—seeing them both dead.

Excerpt 1 from Byzantine Gold

Charlotte answered on the fourth ring. Caller I.D. showed "restricted."

"Hello."

"They are called, Angelique tulips. You admired them in the hospital garden in Paris."

Charlotte froze, holding her breath as she listened to the nightmare voice, remembering how his Eastern European accent rounded certain sounds and how he stressed the last syllables in his words. Called became *cawl-d.*

Tischenko.

"Everything in time," he said and hung up.

Charlotte dropped the phone on the table. She turned to Atakan.

The shock must've shown on her face. "What is wrong?"

"That was Tischenko," she said, finding her voice. "The flowers are from him. He was watching me in Paris when I was at the hospital. He—"

Atakan didn't wait for her to finish. He rushed into the living room, grabbed his gun from the bookshelf, and ran out of the apartment.

Charlotte followed as he flew down the four flights of stairs to the street.

"Stop." Catching up to him on the sidewalk, she hooked his elbow with her hand. Fearful an armed Tischenko hid nearby, she positioned herself in front of

Atakan, thinking to shield him. "We can't stand here. He could be anywhere taking aim at you right now."

"Go back inside."

"Not without you." She tugged on his shirt, pulling him toward their building. "Atakan please, let's leave. Call the Director."

Atakan shoved her behind him. Silent, his eyes searched the dark doorways of neighboring apartment buildings and parked cars.

"Atakan please."

"Get inside."

She stepped in front of him again. "We stay here together or we leave together."

An eternity of seconds passed. Neither moved or blinked.

They both jumped and turned at the bellow from the horn of a passing truck. Thankfully, the driver was waving to another coming the opposite direction. He never saw the man in the sling pointing a gun at him.

"Please," she repeated.

Atakan nodded. He stopped at the building's entry door and took a last look, surveying the street. "He moves us around like pawns in a private game."

Chapter One

Paris-April

Charlotte and Atakan stopped midway on Sacre-Coeur's steep staircase to admire the basilica's architecture. The Romanesque-Byzantine influence reminded her of historical buildings in Istanbul, their home. With the variegated onion-shaped domes and turrets similar to minarets, the church was one of the more unique city structures.

"So beautiful," Charlotte said, "like an artifact on top of the skyline." Atakan hadn't said much as they came up the hill. She wasn't sure if he was impressed or not.

"Reminds me of an Ottoman wedding cake," he replied.

"Seeing this makes me anxious to start the recovery project," Charlotte said, adding, "provided they select me for the team."

"They will."

Atakan embraced her from behind and nuzzled her neck, the uber sensitive side, then rested his chin on her head. She giggled, wrapped her arms around his and pressed deeper into his chest. He rarely showed his romantic side in public. Apparently, the romance of Paris had inspired him. She opened her mouth to say as much, but changed her mind. Why spoil the moment?

"You have a taste for Byzantine style jewelry. The Cyprus shipwreck is from that period. Perhaps we'll get lucky and find a cache of jewelry at the site. You'll have the opportunity to hold authentic pieces." He released his embrace and moved next to her. "Shall we?"

A faint shiver trickled down her spine with the loss of his body's warmth.

They continued to the entrance and inside.

"Let's go to the dome first," Charlotte said.

They climbed the narrow, spiral staircase eighty-three meters to the top, holding hands as they strolled along the gallery enjoying the panoramic sight.

Atakan stopped to study the elegant capitals topping the support columns. "Excellent stonework," he said with is archaeologist's eye for detail.

She leaned over the railing to people watch. Below her, guides led their clusters of tourists to the apse, famous for its golden mosaics and from there to different quiet corners of the basilica to point out the highlights.

"Charlotte, turn around. Smile." Atakan played with the camera in his phone for a few seconds then snapped a photo. "I'll be right back. I want one of the Eiffel Tower and Arc de Triomphe."

She continued to people watch from her birds-eyes view. A lone man in a baseball cap walked up the main aisle. He wore sunglasses in spite of the overcast April sky. He kept his hands in the pockets of his bomber jacket and looked straight ahead, showing no interest in the stain-glass windows or other architectural features.

She turned her attention to the constant stream of worshipers who took seats on pews away from the tour groups. Some knelt and prayed, others sat with eyes closed, their hands folded, and listened to the nuns singing.

A large group of tourists and the lone male approached the chancel, directly below Charlotte. The man stepped aside to allow the guide and her charges to pass. Then, he removed his cap and glasses, looked up at Charlotte, and smiled.

The past terror she'd buried and fought to forget returned with a vengeance. Rocked, she sucked in a fear driven gasp and reflexively jerked back.

She shook off the panic. Angry with herself for the way she reacted and pissed the bastard still had that effect. She peered over the rail again. Maybe she was wrong.

She wasn't. The same brush-cut hair, the same dimpled smile as he kept his eyes on her, the handsome Slavic face was forever etched in her memory...the face of the man who'd kidnapped and tortured her.

Heart pounding, she spun, dashed to where Atakan snapped pictures and grabbed his arm. "Quick, Tischenko is here."

"Charlotte—" He followed as she raced down the twisting staircase. Visitors coming from the other direction flattened themselves to the wall, out of her way and his.

When they reached the main floor, Atakan pushed past her and blocked her path. He held her by the upper arms. "Charlotte, stop for a moment. Where did you see him?"

She tried to pull away. "Here—he was walking down the center aisle," she stressed, searching the faces in the crowd of visitors.

Tischenko was gone.

"I tell you, I saw him."

Atakan continued to hold onto her as he scanned the aisles and pews. "I don't see anyone resembling him, let alone the man himself."

"He must've realized we'd chase after him. Come on, he can't have gone far." She broke from Atakan and hurried along the aisle with the fewest tourists and out the doors.

She hesitated on the portico. The ever-present musician buskers with their open instrument cases and people resting from the long climb littered the stairs.

Her eyes darted from one person to the next. "He's wearing a black leather jacket and ball cap. He's not here. Which way do you think he went?" she asked, turning to Atakan. "Maybe the metro—Abbesses is the closest stop."

"If I were running from a wild woman, I wouldn't risk getting caught at a station waiting for a train."

"I bet he ran through the gardens toward Place Saint-Pierre." She glanced at her watch. "Almost noon. The square will be swarming with families and lunchtime diners, easy to blend in and get lost."

She threaded her way through the crowd toward Saint-Pierre. Ahead, a fair-haired man, in a black leather jacket walked at a brisk pace by the merry-go-round playing a tinny version of the *Star Wars Theme*. Jogging faster, Charlotte caught up to him and yanked on his arm.

The man looked momentarily stunned.

Not Tischenko.

"Pardon monsieur," Atakan apologized and took Charlotte aside. "Enough!"

"I—"

"Enough."

"I'd swear—"

"It was not him at the church."

She hadn't thought of Tischenko in months. How likely was it for her to imagine seeing him? But if it was him, he did a great job of vaporizing.

She laid her head on Atakan's shoulder for a long moment. He rubbed her back along the spine until the adrenaline rush passed and she calmed.

"You're hungry," she said at last, hearing his stomach rumble. "Le Barouder is charming and nearby."

"No. We're not eating anywhere in Montmartre. I don't want to be in the middle of my food and have to chase after you because you think you've seen Tischenko again. We'll find a café by the hotel."

"Pretend for a minute, I'm right. It's—"

"*If* it's true, his presence here is a coincidence."

"You don't believe in coincidence."

"In this case, I do." Atakan bent and brushed her lips with a light kiss. "So intelligent and lovely, a pity you are crazy."

"That's what makes life with me exciting," she said, with feigned, wide-eyed innocence.

"I'm not sure exciting is the right word."

Still uneasy, Charlotte scanned the crowd one last time.

Across the square, Maksym Tischenko stepped from the rear of the crepe vendor's stall. Atakan and the Dashiell woman returned the way they came. Maksym took side streets that didn't intersect with the one Atakan and Dashiell were on. At the main avenue, he hailed a cab and instructed the driver to take him to Hotel Du Danube, where the couple was staying.

Excerpt 2 from Byzantine Gold

Charlotte answered on the fourth ring. Caller I.D. showed "restricted."

"Hello."

"They are called, Angelique tulips. You admired them in the hospital garden in Paris."

Charlotte froze, holding her breath as she listened to the nightmare voice, remembering how his Eastern European accent rounded certain sounds and how he stressed the last syllables in his words. Called became *cawl-d*.

Tischenko.

"Everything in time," he said and hung up.

Charlotte dropped the phone on the table. She turned to Atakan.

The shock must've shown on her face. "What is wrong?"

"That was Tischenko," she said, finding her voice. "The flowers are from him. He was watching me in Paris when I was at the hospital. He—"

Atakan didn't wait for her to finish. He rushed into the living room, grabbed his gun from the bookshelf, and ran out of the apartment.

Charlotte followed as he flew down the four flights of stairs to the street.

"Stop." Catching up to him on the sidewalk, she hooked his elbow with her hand. Fearful an armed Tischenko hid nearby, she positioned herself in front of

Atakan, thinking to shield him. "We can't stand here. He could be anywhere taking aim at you right now."

"Go back inside."

"Not without you." She tugged on his shirt, pulling him toward their building. "Atakan please, let's leave. Call the Director."

Atakan shoved her behind him. Silent, his eyes searched the dark doorways of neighboring apartment buildings and parked cars.

"Atakan please."

"Get inside."

She stepped in front of him again. "We stay here together or we leave together."

An eternity of seconds passed. Neither moved or blinked.

They both jumped and turned at the bellow from the horn of a passing truck. Thankfully, the driver was waving to another coming the opposite direction. He never saw the man in the sling pointing a gun at him.

"Please," she repeated.

Atakan nodded. He stopped at the building's entry door and took a last look, surveying the street. "He moves us around like pawns in a private game."

Excerpt 3 from Byzantine Gold

Charlotte's worries regarding telling Atakan the truth and the negative dive with Nassor pressed on her mind. Tired to the bone, she headed for the women's dorm to drop her backpack. From there, she couldn't wait to shower. Maybe standing under the hot water would clear her head and she'd know how to approach Atakan.

She was almost at the dorm when the cook's truck came to a quick stop next to her. Atakan was behind the wheel. He leaned across the cab of the truck and flung open the passenger door.

"Get in."

"Now? I wanted to take a shower. How about I meet you in twenty minutes?"

"Get in," he said, flatly.

Charlotte tossed her backpack in the truck bed and climbed into the passenger seat. He pulled away before she had the door completely closed.

"Where are we going?" she asked, shutting the door.

Atakan didn't answer as he sped out of camp, spraying dirt and stones behind them.

"What's going on? Why are you in such a hurry?"

He stared straight ahead, silent.

"Atakan?"

Tight-jawed, he continued down the side road

that paralleled the beach, ramming the stick shift into place as he went through the gears and ignoring her questions. She'd never seen him this tense, not with her at least. A bad feeling crept over her. She had a sick sense his mood involved her plan to leave.

They'd gone a kilometer from the camp when he came to a stop. He hopped out, slammed the driver's door shut and came to her side.

Opening her door, he said, "Get out."

She did.

"Atakan," Charlotte started to ask the same questions again, but he was already turned and walking toward the sea.

She followed. He finally stopped near the water's edge with his back to the surf and faced her. She stopped a couple of yards away.

"When were you going to tell me?"

She knew exactly what he was asking about. Who told him? It wasn't Nick. He'd honor the twenty-four hour rule.

"Who told you?"

"That's not an answer." He stood still as a statue, arms crossed, feet apart.

She hesitated, trying to choose her words so he'd understand and not be hurt. She gazed out at the incoming tide. The blue-green waves, effervescent with bubbles, rushed toward shore in rapid succession. White foam droplets filled the air as they crested, framing him like a new, angry version of Poseidon.

"Answer me."

"Today."

"You weren't going to tell me until today, although you've been planning to leave me for awhile."

"Not awhile."

"Long enough to send job inquiries to several museums."

So that was how he knew. One of the museums contacted MIAR and they must've sent the questionnaire to Refik and he told Atakan. She hadn't considered the possibility. She'd thought any contact from the museums would be handled by MIAR's headquarters.

"I'm so sorry you had to find out this way. I intended to tell you if it looked like I'd definitely leave. If none of the museums showed interest, then you never had to know what I'd done."

"And you believe that is acceptable?"

It killed her to see the look of disgust on his face with the question. "Yes..." she said low.

"Why?"

"Because I'm bad luck for you—everyone can see it, even your--, it's obvious. There's something about me, and God knows, I don't know what, but I'm like a magnet for Tischenko."

She never cried and she wouldn't cry now, but she was close. "I can't bear to see you hurt again, or worse. There are people that bad luck follows, even Iskender thinks so."

Atakan inhaled deeply and let out a slow breath. Uncrossing his arms, he closed the short distance to where she stood.

"It's not forever," she offered, "I'll return."

He shook his head. "If you go, you cannot return. You're either in my life or out of my life. There's no in between."

5.0 out of 5 stars **Action packed with a little steam**,

This review is from: Byzantine Gold (Dangerous Waters) (Kindle Edition)

Like other reviewers said, this is a thriller with stellar action that keeps the reader turning pages well into the night. I thoroughly enjoyed the action and excitement, but what I enjoyed more was getting to know Charlotte and Atakan from the previous book, Golden Chariot better. They were such an interesting couple and I was glad Karlsen brought them back for this book. I liked seeing their relationship now after they've been together for a year. As for Tischenko, the killer from book one, Karlsen has fleshed him out well. At times, he's almost, almost the villain you hate to love.

Byzantine Gold is another winner for Karlsen!!

Karlsen has another winner

This review is from: Byzantine Gold (Dangerous Waters) (Kindle Edition)

An action packed sequel to Chris Karlsen's Golden Chariot! You'll love the way she weaved her story together with old world history and current events. I enjoyed reading more about Charlotte and Atakan and getting the resolution of a past situation that involved Atakan's arch nemesis Tischenko. Romantic suspense at its best!

Even better than the first book!,

This review is from: Byzantine Gold (Dangerous Waters) (Kindle Edition)

As expected, this book did not disappoint. We still have the same lovely archaeological awesomeness we encountered in Golden Chariot. I accidentally learned stuff and I wasn't bored. ;) There is still the lovely romance going on between Charlotte and Atakan. It is still progressing and I still love the mess out of these two characters. They are from different cultures and they clash but I love their banter and Charlotte's teasing. They are so great together. One of my complaints from the last book was that we could not get into Atakan's head. (: I am proud to announce that that cannot be said about this book! I was so excited to continue the hunt for the bad guy from the first book. There was some unresolved conflict and it was tackled head on in this sequel. We still get our different POVs from the main characters and the "villians". When it comes to murder mysteries and bad guys, that is a MUST for getting both sides of the story and getting to know the bad guy as well. hehe. The underwater dives and communications between the two main characters was one of my favorite aspects from the first book, so it was great to see more of that. I love love love how they friendship is still evolving! (: Gah, those two. And Atakan has this kind of hot macho man vibe. *wiggles eyebrows* And Charlotte is no simpering weakling either, as we learned in the first book. You know you love that in your badass Suspense/Action heroes! This sequel definitely did not disappoint. (: I love romantic suspense and Golden Chariot definitely fits the bill for a great Book filled with action, adventure, romance.. and suspense!! Also... the covers for both of these books are fantastic. I could not even fathom another cover for this series.

RECIPES FROM CHRIS KARLSEN:

Toward the end of **Heroes Live Forever**, Miranda invites Ian to dinner and serves **Beef Stroganoff**.

I still have an old-fashioned cork recipe board. I have a stroganoff recipe pinned to it that I've had for years and years. I clipped it from a magazine but no longer remember which magazine so I cannot offer the source. I can only say, I've made this recipe and enjoyed it.

Beef Stroganoff:

¼ cup butter

¼ cup flour

1 lb. tenderloin tips or tri-tip cubed

½ cup onion, diced

1 clove garlic, minced

1 cup sliced mushrooms

1 can beef consommé

¼ cup dry sherry

1 cup sour cream

Paprika

Put meat in bag of flour and shake to dust cubes. Sauté in butter the onion and garlic for a few minutes, then add the meat and mushrooms and lightly brown. Stir in consommé and cook over low heat for about 20 minutes. Add sherry and sour cream, stir and cook another 5 minutes. Sprinkle with paprika (if desired) and serve over noodles.

In one scene in **Journey in Time**, Alex is going to cook for Shakira. The dish isn't mentioned but he does

ask her to make a salad. My husband and I prefer homemade dressings to bottle/prepared ones. A favorite in our house comes from Emeril Lagasse. It is a
Dijon/vinaigrette
  1 Tbl. Dijon mustard
  2 tsp. Shallots
  2 tsp. champagne vinegar
  3 Tbl. Canola oil or vegetable oil (we use canola)
  1 Tbl. Extra virgin olive oil
  Pinch of salt

**I like to add pickled beets to our salads. They're a favorite of my husband's. I mix red beets with the yellow ones for the color. I use the pickling recipe my mother gave me. Where she got it from years ago, she doesn't know. She believes from my grandmother

  Pickling Spice:
  1 red onion
  1 cup rice wine vinegar
  1 ½ tsp salt
  ½ cup water

Slice the beets and put them in a jar with a lid. Pour the liquid over the beets and place in refrigerator for 7 days before serving.

In **Knight Blindness**, book three in my Knights in Time series, Alex, the hero of Journey in Time who loves to cook, prepares **beef bourguignon** for Stephen the wounded hero of Knight Blindness.

This recipe was given to me by a dear friend and fabulous chef, the late Manny Zwaaf. One evening when we were his dinner guests, he prepared this dish. I loved it and asked for the recipe. Like so many chefs, he told me he never measures. The measurements are the best-guess-estimate I use

Beef Bourguignon:

Tri-tip roast (I use a 2 ½ to 3 lb. roast) with fat removed and cubed. Place meat in plastic bowl.

Salt & Pepper to taste

Add red wine (I use about a ½ cup)

Cut onions (I like one medium)

Carrots (I use about a cup of baby carrots peeled)

Thyme (tsp)

Couple of bay leaves, sprig of parsley, little rosemary,

Little olive oil (for me about 1/3 cup of oil is good). This is a marinade so I try not to overuse any ingredient.

Cover the bowl with plastic wrap or lid and refrigerate for two days, turn occasionally.

**After two days, remove from fridge, drain marinade through colander and sauté the remains. Brown the meat and put both into large pot.

On top of meat, place 1-2 Tbl tomato paste, mix 1-2 Tbl flour, mix without heat into marinade and put marinade back on top. Add one can of beef bouillon with a spoon of beef paste (I like to add an extra spoon of the paste). Mix together and put on a very low flame, cover and stir as needed.

If liquid is too thin, remove cover. When meat is done, let pot stand for one day. When you reheat, add a little more wine with a shot of brandy and a spoon of sugar.

**I don't usually let it stand for a day, although I know I should. I tend to serve it that night over mashed potatoes or noodles.

Final recipe:

In Byzantine Gold, Charlotte and Atakan are preparing an eggplant and rice veggie dish in one scene. They live in Istanbul as Atakan is a government agent and this is the Turkish recipe I have for the dish. This is from a book I bought on a trip to Istanbul: Turkish Cookery distributed by Net Books.

Patlicanli Pilav

Basmati rice (prepare according to package
2 medium onions (chopped)
2 medium tomatoes (peeled and chopped)
½ cup olive oil/1 lb. eggplant
1 Tbl pine nuts
1 Tbl currants
1 tsp cinnamon
1 tsp allspice
2 tsp salt
4 tsp sugar

½ tsp fresh ground pepper
Bunch of fresh dill

Peel eggplants and cut lengthwise into four strips then cube. Soak them in salted water for about 15-20 minutes. Then drain, dry and sauté to lightly brown in olive oil. Remove when done.

In same pan, put chopped onions and pine nuts. Brown them on medium heat. Add the rice and brown for another 10 minutes, stirring constantly. Add tomatoes, salt, pepper, sugar, currants, fried eggplants and 1 ½ to 2 cups water. Cover and simmer on low heat for 20 minutes.

Mix well before serving. Garnish with dill.

ABOUT THE AUTHOR

I was born and raised in Chicago. My father was a history professor and my mother was, and is, a voracious reader. I grew up with a love of history and books. My parents also love traveling, a passion they passed onto me. I wanted to see the places I read about, see the land and monuments from the time periods that fascinated me. I've had the good fortune to travel extensively throughout Europe, the Near East, and North Africa.

I am a retired police detective. I spent twenty-five years in law enforcement with two different agencies. My desire to write came in my early teens. After I retired, I decided to pursue that dream. I write two different series. My paranormal romance series is called, Knights in Time. My romantic thriller series is, Dangerous Waters.

I currently live in the Pacific Northwest with my husband, four rescue dogs and a rescue horse.

Best-selling Books

Made in the USA
Charleston, SC
05 January 2014